qE   76-2716

Hoban
    A near thing for Cap-
tain Najork

Russell Hoban

A Near Thing for Captain Najork

Illustrated by Quentin Blake

Atheneum 1976 New York

Also by Russell Hoban and Quentin Blake

HOW TOM BEAT CAPTAIN NAJORK AND HIS HIRED SPORTSMEN

1659733

Library of Congress Cataloging in Publication Data

Hoban, Russell.

   A near thing for Captain Najork.

   SUMMARY: Tom finds that he can beat Captain Najork
and his hired sportsmen at more than games.
   I. Blake, Quentin. II. Title.
PZ7.H637Ne [E] 75-29464
ISBN 0-689-30503-6

One morning after breakfast Tom was fooling around with his chemistry set and he invented anti-sticky.

Then he fooled around with anti-sticky and jam and
springs and wheels and connecting-rods and he made a
two-seater jam-powered frog.

Tom got into the frog with Aunt Bundlejoy Cosysweet and started it up. The frog hopped over the fence and the next three gardens in one giant hop.

"What makes it go?" said Aunt Bundlejoy.
"Jam," said Tom. "When the anti-sticky
plate hits the sticky it bounces back.
The spring keeps it going, the connecting-
rods move up and down, the wheels go
round and the frog hops."

Tom and Aunt Bundlejoy took the frog
out for a spin.

They hopped along the river and they hopped past
Aunt Fidget Wonkham-Strong Najork's house.

Captain Najork was in the observatory looking through his telescope at the girls' boarding-school across the river when the frog hopped past.

"Follow that frog!" he shouted to his hired sportsmen as he leapt into his pedal-powered snake, and away they undulated. Captain Najork had not forgotten the time when Tom had beaten him and his hired sportsmen at womble, muck, and sneedball. "I'd like to try some new games on him," said the Captain. "I'd like to see how good he is at thud, crunch, and Tom-on-the-bottom."

Aunt Fidget Wonkham-Strong Najork came up the observatory stairs singing 'Heart of Oak'. She had tea and scones for the Captain's elevenses but he was not there.

She looked out of the window and saw that the Captain's snake was gone.

She looked through the telescope and saw the Headmistress of the girls' boarding-school practising two-handed clean-and-jerks with her bar-bells. "Aha!" said Aunt Fidget Wonkham-Strong Najork.

She put on her flippers and snorkel, swam the river,
and knocked at the girls' boarding-school door.
    "Can I help you, madam?" said the commissionaire.
    Aunt Fidget Wonkham-Strong Najork knocked him
down and went straight to the Headmistress's office.

"Where is the Captain?" she said.

"Of which team?" said the Headmistress. "Hockey, squash, or lacrosse?"

"You know whom I mean," said Aunt Fidget Wonkham-Strong Najork. "Produce him instantly."

"You're dripping on my carpet," said the Headmistress.

"Very well," said Aunt Fidget Wonkham-Strong Najork. "I will arm-wrestle you for Captain Najork. Best out of three."

. . . Tom and Aunt Bundlejoy hopped on in the jam-powered frog.

"We're being followed by a five-seater snake," said Aunt Bundlejoy.

"That must be Captain Najork," said Tom. "Does he want to race?"

"I think he wants to swallow us," said Aunt Bundlejoy. "The snake has got its mouth wide open."

"Bad luck," said Tom. "We're running out of sticky and I've left the jam at home."

"They're bound to have pots of jam at the girls' boarding-school," said Aunt Bundlejoy.

Tom turned the frog around and away they went back up the river with the snake only a few frog-lengths behind.

"You beat us at womble!" shouted the Captain. "You beat us at muck and sneedball! But you won't win this time!"

Tom and Aunt Bundlejoy barely cleared the boarding-school wall with the frog's last hop.

Aunt Bundlejoy knocked on the door.
   "Can I help you, madam?" said
the commissionaire.
   "Our frog's out of jam," said Aunt Bundlejoy.
   "Can you lend us a pot?"
   "Just a moment, please," said
the commissionaire. "I'll have
to ask the Headmistress for the keys
to the jam locker."

As the commissionaire came into the Headmistress's office
he saw the head of Captain Najork's snake at the open window.

"There is a lady at the door who wants a pot of jam and there
is a snake at the window, madam," he said.

"I can't be interrupted now," said the headmistress. "Ask
them to wait."

When Aunt Fidget Wonkham-Strong Najork saw the snake
she was so cross with the Captain that she flung the Headmistress
through the window into the snake's open mouth.

"Oy!" said the Captain. He stepped on the ejector-pedal and the Headmistress shot back through the window and flattened Aunt Fidget Wonkham-Strong Najork. As his wife's feet flew up, Captain Najork recognized her flippers.

"May I have my wife please?" he said to the commissionaire.
The commissionaire handed Aunt Fidget Wonkham-Strong Najork out to the Captain and he put her on the sofa in the snake's lounge.

"I think we had better go home now," he said to the hired sportsmen, and they undulated back over the wall and away.

Now that she'd seen Captain Najork
the Headmistress had taken a fancy to him.
"After them!" she shouted to Tom and
Aunt Bundlejoy. "We haven't finished
arm-wrestling!"
"We're out of jam," said Tom.
A pot of jam was quickly fetched and
they hopped off after the snake.

They caught up with it at the landing-stage by Aunt Fidget
Wonkham-Strong Najork's house.

As the Captain was helping his wife ashore the Headmistress
leapt out of the frog and plucked at Aunt Fidget Wonkham-
Strong Najork's sleeve.

"That's quite all right," said Aunt Fidget Wonkham-Strong Najork. "No explanations are necessary. The Captain has convinced me that my suspicions were unfounded."

"Never mind that," said the Headmistress. "You said best out of three and we haven't even finished one."

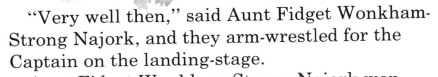

"Very well then," said Aunt Fidget Wonkham-
Strong Najork, and they arm-wrestled for the
Captain on the landing-stage.

Aunt Fidget Wonkham-Strong Najork won
twice in a row and the Headmistress wept
bitter tears.

"The Captain would have lent such an air to the establishment!" she said.

"Did you want to play some more games?" said Tom to the Captain.

"He can't," said Aunt Fidget Wonkham-Strong Najork.

"He's got to have his lunch and he'll be learning off pages of the Nautical Almanac for the rest of the day."

"Eat your swede-and-mutton slump," said Aunt Fidget
Wonkham-Strong Najork to the Captain. "And think
how lucky you are to be here. That was a near thing
for you today."

"Yes, dear," said the Captain. He ate it.